Rocky the Lighthouse Makes a Difference

Written and Illustrated
By Jeffrey Noel

Copyright @ 2008 by Jeffrey Noel

All rights reserved.

No part of this book may be reproduced without written permission from the publisher or copyright holders, except for a reviewer who may quote brief passages in a review; nor may any part of this book be reproduced, stored in a retrieval system, or transmitted in any form or by any means electronic, mechanical, photocopying, recording or other, without written permission from the publisher or copyright holder.

Robert D. Reed Publishers
P.O. Box 1992
Bandon, OR 97411
Phone: (541) 347-9882; Fax: -9883
Email: 4bobreed@msn.com
Website: www.rdrpublishers.com

Illustrator: Jeffrey Noel
Cover Designer: Cleone Lyvonne
Typesetter/Graphic Designer: Katherine Hyde

Special Acknowledgment: Some illustrated characters based on an untitled placemat from a restauarant.

ISBN: 978-1-931741-93-4

Produced and manufactured under the direction of
Double Eagle Industries
For manufacturing details, call 888-824-4344

Printed in China

For Susan

Rocky stands alone at the edge of the coast and watches the sea. His smile brightens the sky in the day and the night. He might seem plain at first, but if you look closer . . .

Rocky is a very special lighthouse. Every day his bright smile shines across the water. He makes many friends in his role as protector of travelers and light of the coast. Fishes, mussels, tourists, seamen, starfish and stars are all his friends.

He wanted to make a difference and to help someone. People would come from miles away to see him and his light. He had his own source of light that did not rely on anything external.

At night, Rocky passes the time by talking to the stars in the heavens twinkling. It's no wonder they became friends; both are steady and bright. He always lets them know how glad he is to have someone to keep him company during the long nights when everyone is sleeping.

Sometimes Rocky sings to the stars to keep them company.

Shine your light a little while
Show your friends a happy smile
Shine your light around the sky
Don't be bashful, don't be shy

Sometimes they just twinkled at each other in silence, shining brightly, happy to know they were all sharing the night together.

On a dark night Rocky could watch the glow from the trails of the passing boats as tiny sea creatures created light when the ships stirred the waters where they lived. The moon looked on happily with approval as Rocky kept watch.

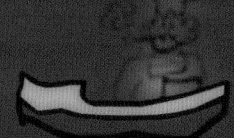

Time goes by slowly and Rocky doesn't know if anyone needs him. He has many friends, but Rocky wonders if he really makes a difference. Do people notice him doing his job every day? He works hard to make sure his light is always shining brightly. Tourists visit him often, but is he just an antique? He prepares for bad weather and darkness, but nothing interesting ever happens.

Rocky would sound his horn so people could hear him. He sometimes would run out of breath and get frustrated, thinking that no one heard him. "No one ever answers me."

One day Rocky overheard the tour guide talking about his light. "These old things are really just relics now. It is the modern age of navigation with electronics and satellites. Lighthouses are really not necessary."

Rocky was heartbroken and saddened when he heard the tour guide. Maybe Rocky only heard part of the story. Nonetheless, he questioned his purpose and reason for being.

Rocky stayed up all the long nights and nothing ever happened, so he told the stars he was going to go to sleep at night now like everyone else. What difference would it make if he just kept his light inside himself?

Rocky said, "It is the age of modern navigation. Nobody needs an old lighthouse, and I could use some rest."

Then the stars said, "Why not shine your light for everyone to see? The stars are hidden in the day. People only know us at night, but you can be seen and heard any time. How fortunate you are to be able to talk freely to people and to help them every day. Only on a clear night can we help people." But Rocky didn't listen to the stars.

Rocky grew tired and asked himself why he bothered to shine his light and sound his horn. He stopped smiling, closed his eyes and thought for a while.

Rocky slept the days and nights away and snored softly with his foghorn. Rocky's friends all missed him. The world seemed less joyful without Rocky's bright smile, but they all agreed they should just carry on without him.

Then one night there was a tremendous storm.

Many ships and captains are lost and afraid of this nasty storm. They are adrift and being tossed about by the waves and wind. They fear the rocks near the shore that they can no longer see in the dark. A lightning bolt hit one of the ships and knocked out the radio and all of the fancy navigation electronics.

The ship's captain, Captain Crabby, regretted the untimely loss of his fancy electronic equipment. Fearing the loss of his ship, his crew, and his life, he remained at the wheel, trembling in the cold rain. He was determined to find a way to get his ship and crew home safely.

"See if you can get a fix on the city or the stars to help us navigate to safety," he shouted to his crew. There were no lights in the city and no stars visible through the storm clouds.

Rocky wakes up to a tremendous splash and his feet are all wet. There is a horrible storm, and he cannot find his friends the stars. He has never been so alone and afraid. He is worried that the storm might hurt someone.

Rocky tries to talk to his friends, the stars, but he cannot see them. He gets more and more afraid. He took his friends for granted and thought that they would always be there for him. Where had they gone?

Finally, he heard a faint answer to his foghorn cries. The faint reply did not come from up in the sky. It came from his foundation. He looked down, but could not see anything. He thought he heard, "Rocky—shine your light for all to see." The storm was getting louder and louder, and even the lights in the city to the west were dark. Lightning must have knocked out the power in the city.

Then he heard the sound again. But he did not see anything. . . . He looked again and he saw a small light below him.

"Rocky—it is me—down here—Susan Starfish. I know the stars in the heavens and they are still there. You just can't see them. Lots of things are like that in life. The storm clouds are just too thick to see through."

"You have to keep shining your light even if you don't think anyone notices you. That is how you make a difference, a little bit at a time. It doesn't matter if people don't notice you every single day, because they will notice when they need you."

Susan Starfish struggled to fight off the waves while she shouted encouragement to Rocky with all her breath.

Rocky noticed the glowing object below and was puzzled. He said, "But you are a starfish. How can you make light? You are not like the stars in the sky."

Although it was dark and uncomfortable, Susan Starfish laughed out loud and said, "Everyone has their own way of shining—watch this!" and with all her strength she spun very fast through the seawater until there was a greenish-yellow light glowing from her arms. She shouted, out of breath, "It's called phosphorescence* or bioluminescence."

*(Big word but sounds like FOS-FOR-ES-ENS)

"My arms rub on tiny creatures in the water called plankton, and they light up. By themselves, the plankton are too tiny to see, but when they light up all together like fireflies, they can make a bright light on a dark night.
Pretty cool, isn't it?"

Susan Starfish finally asked, "Why are you covering your light? It is so beautiful."

Rocky shines his light down on Susan Starfish and sees how powerfully bright he is and how beautiful Susan is with the glimmer reflecting from her textured starfish skin. Rocky thought about his joyful days and nights when he proudly lit up the coast, and it made him smile brightly. He remembered when he did

What plankton looks like magnified

Plankton are microscopic plant life that are known to make light for many reasons, one of which being mechanical stimulation

not worry about what other people thought about his purpose in life. Rocky just did what he loved. He realized that what the tour guide thought about Rocky's purpose had no real connection to his own idea of lasting happiness. Rocky opened his eyes again and smiled brightly. On that darkest night, his joyful twinkle lit up the sea all around as never before. He no longer feared the storm because he felt calm, warm, and bright inside just like he did on the outside. The angry storm did not take away from the peace he felt in his heart. Susan Starfish saw his light just in time to duck a wave and hang onto Rocky's foundation.

As Rocky opened his eyes and smiled brightly, he lit up the sea for miles around. Captain Crabby looked up from the wheel and said, "Holy smokes! I have never seen such a bright light. That light is from the Rocky Shoals lighthouse. Holy smokes! There is a big rock in front of our ship, lads. Hard to port! Full steam ahead!"

Thanks to Rocky's light, Captain Crabby avoided the rocks and was able to ride out the storm and return home safely.

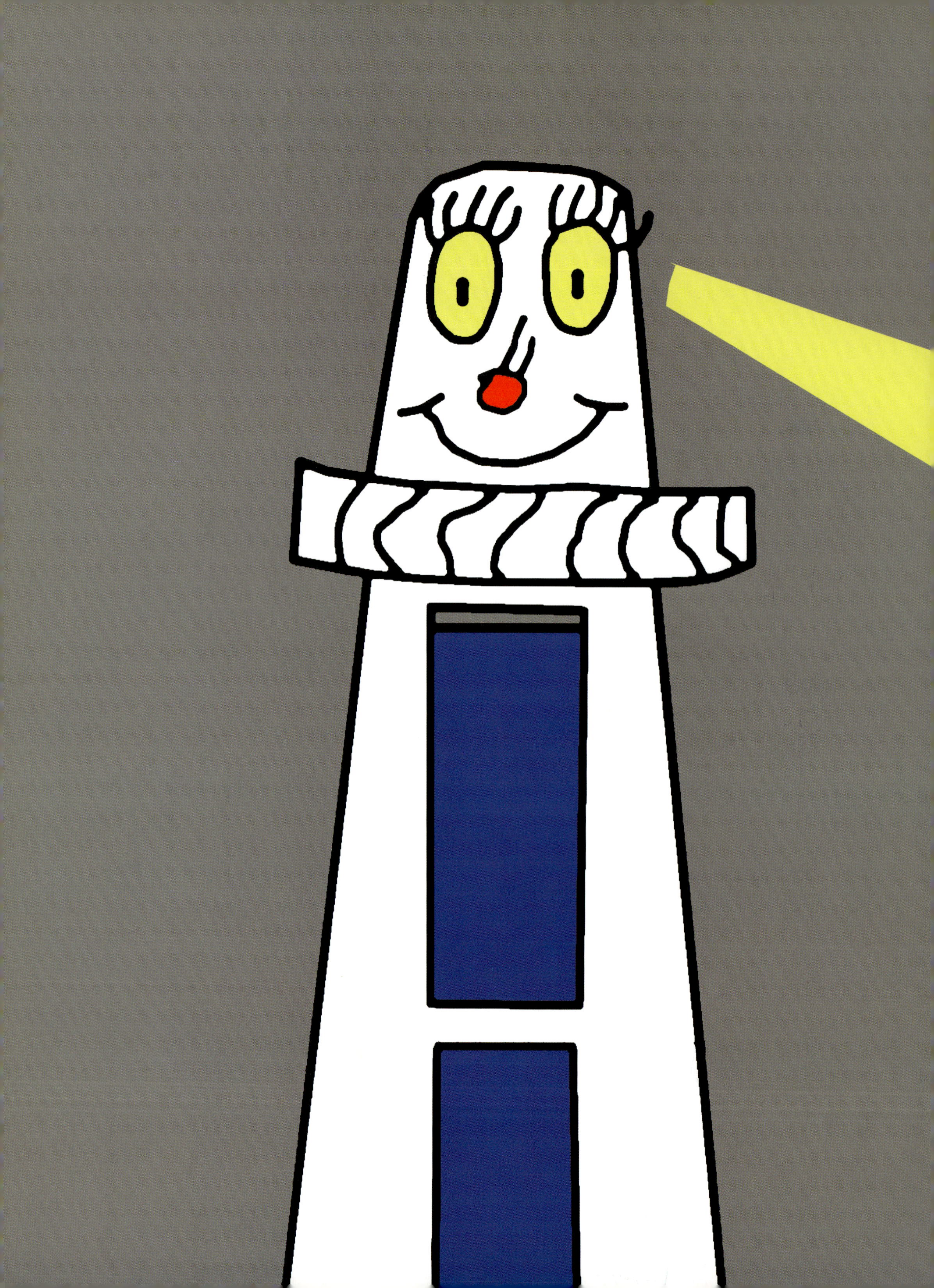

Rocky looked out to sea just in time
to notice Captain Crabby gliding safely
past the rocks. Rocky twinkled again, realizing
he had helped someone even when he was not trying.
He was just shining his light because he realized that was
what he was born to do. He now wondered, why cover his light
when he can let it shine for everyone else to see? The stars were
right all along, and so was Susan Starfish.

The next day was a beautiful clear day, and he visited with all of his old friends the fishes, mussels, tourists, and seamen. Then that night he sang to the stars with his foghorn. Rocky realized he had always been happy and he just got distracted. Susan Starfish told him that he helped her see the waves and hang onto his foundation. Rocky thanked Susan for reminding him of his purpose and that he didn't have to worry about making a big difference all at once. She hugged him and smiled.

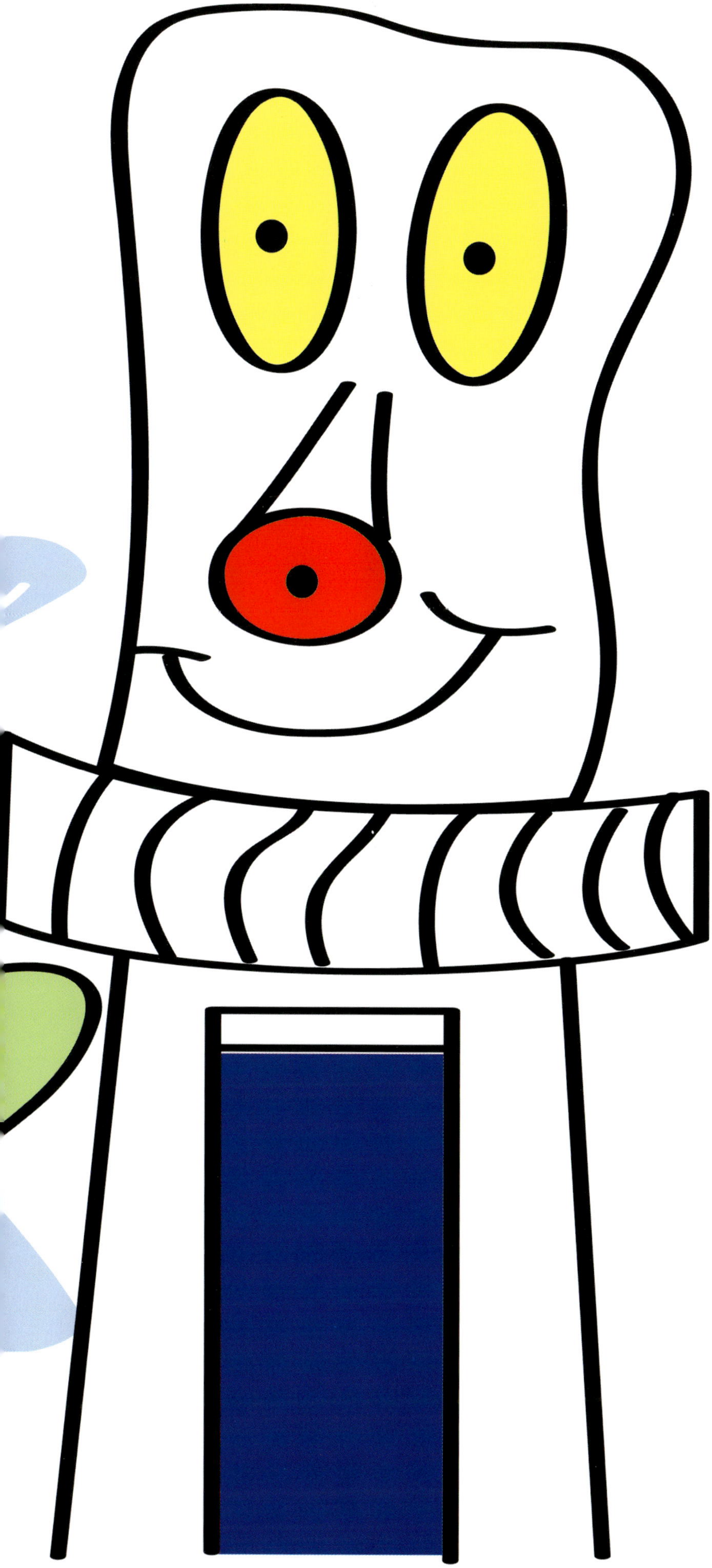

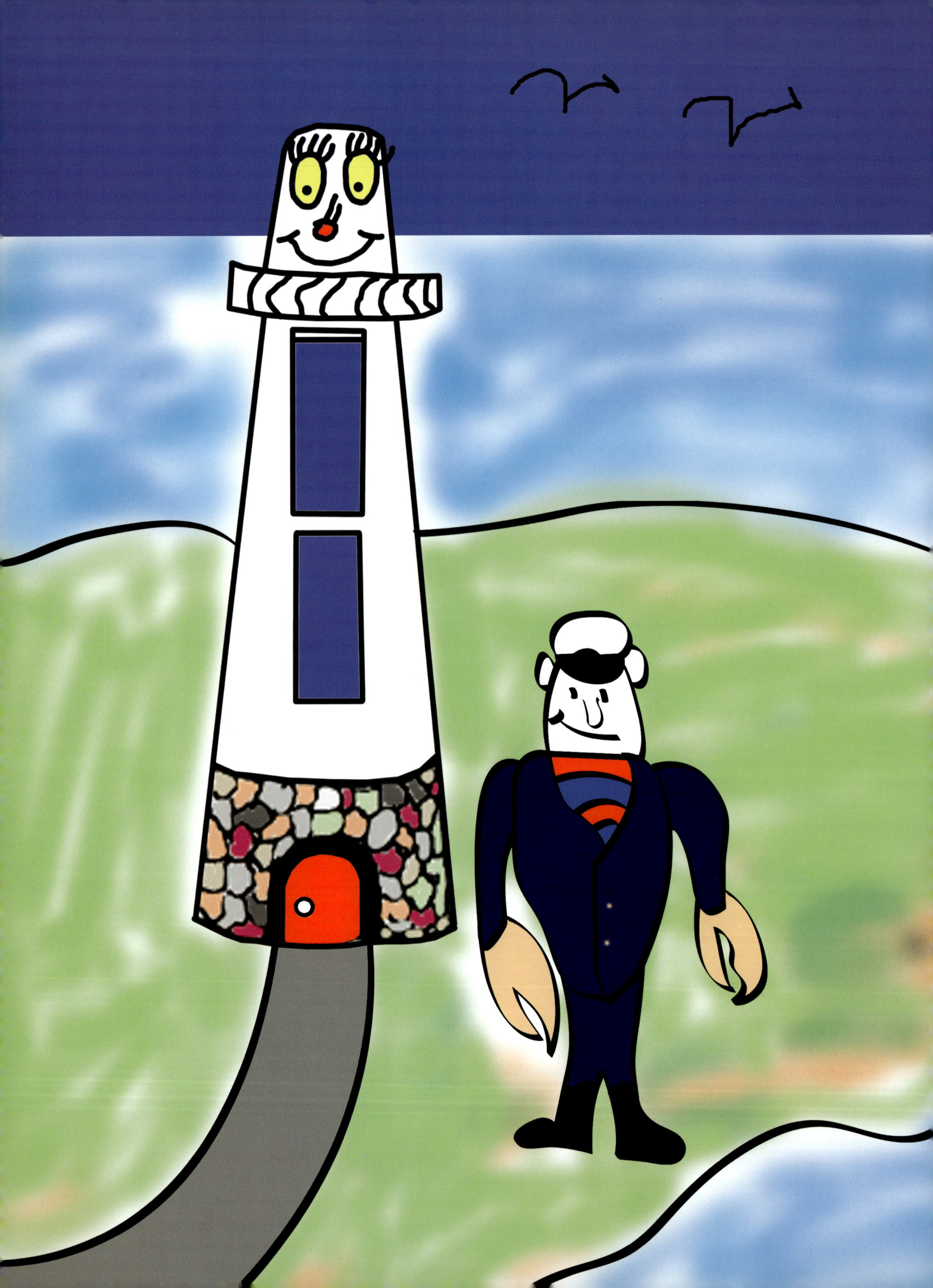

Captain Crabby came by to see him and kiss his rocky foundation. "Rocky, that is the tenth time you saved me and my ship in these past years, so I thought it was about time I came by and thanked you personally. Sorry I never said thank you before, but I guess they don't call me Captain Crabby for nothin'."

Rocky was amazed and had no idea that his light had such an impact on Captain Crabby's illustrious shipping career. He also knew that they really called him Captain Crabby because he had crab claws instead of hands.

Later Rocky heard Captain Crabby tell the tour guide, "This light is special because it is built on a solid foundation and does its job no matter what challenges the weather brings."

"When everything else failed me, Rocky was there for me. I sailed by this lighthouse every day for eighteen years and hardly paid any attention. Then one night he was all I could see. Now I hardly think about anything else when I sail by Rocky Shoals, because this lighthouse saved my life many times. I also know many skippers, including my old friends, Captain Seahorse and Commodore Crusty, who have been guided to safety by this light. We are all proud of Rocky and grateful for his faithful service."

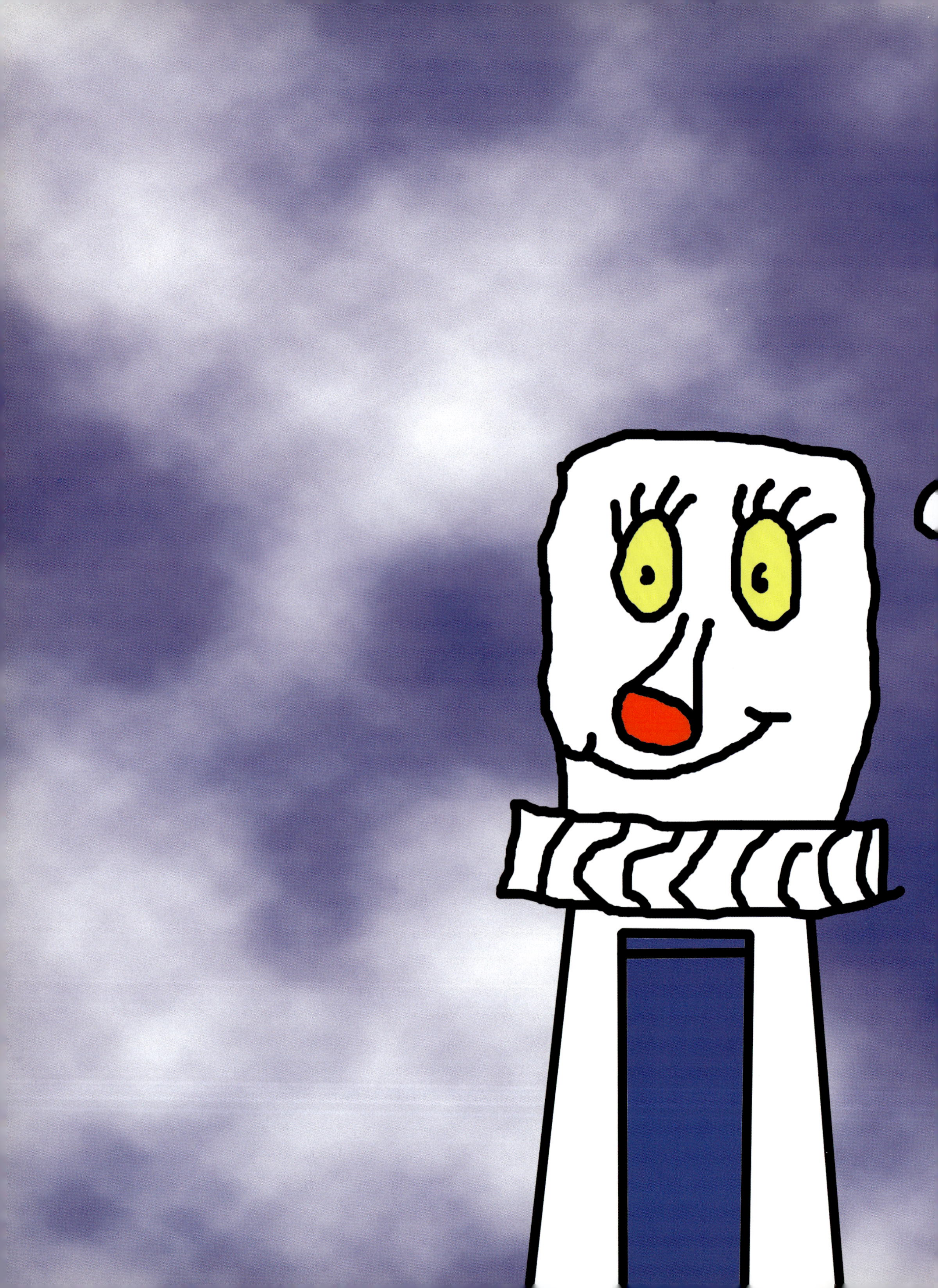

Upon hearing Captain Crabby, Rocky realizes that his smile does help others and he always was noticed. Life is for enjoying what you love, and Rocky's love was guarding the coast and protecting his friends. He just had to stand true to his purpose. The storm revealed to him that he did make a difference after all. He made a big difference on a nasty stormy night because he was reminded by Susan Starfish to shine his light no matter what happens. She said, "Be yourself and do what you love."

CNT uR BLSI

Rocky now knew he always had made a difference, even on the most beautiful sunny day, when he brought joy to his friends through all the little things he did, and on the most beautiful nights when he sang to the stars with his foghorn:

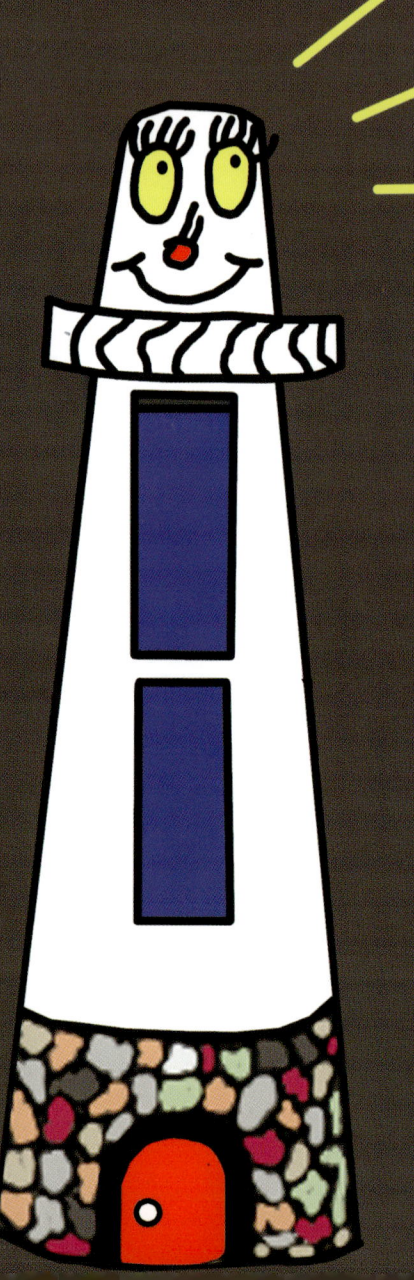

Shine your light a little while
Show your friends a happy smile
Dark clouds sometimes come around
You don't need to wear a frown
Have no fear to get involved
There's lots of problems to be solved
Bit by bit you find your way
Be yourself, don't go astray
To make a difference you'll agree
And shine your light for all to see!

And the stars blessed him with their precious silence and twinkling. Rocky twinkled right back at them!

The End

"A city that is set on a hill cannot be hid. Neither do men light a candle and put it under a bushel."

Matthew 5:14–15

This book is dedicated with love to the philosophy of Susan Holmes Noel. Those who knew her and many that didn't are still blessed by her gifts.

"Sometimes life is rocky and we are shaken by difficulties, but if we stand true to our purpose, our foundation, something happens which reveals that—yes, we do make a difference!"

Susan Carroll Holmes-Noel (1962–2003)